MW01254488

Fog
Gorgeous
Stag

Publishing Genius
1818 E Lafayette Ave
Baltimore, MD 21213
www.publishinggenius.com

ISBN 13: 978-0-9831706-2-4
Cover painting by Chie Fueki
Book design by Adam Robinson

First edition
June 2011

Works in this book originally appeared in *elimae, NANO Fiction, Diagram,*
>kill author and *The Pedestal Magazine.*

Fog Gorgeous Stag

Sean Lovelace

Publishing Genius
Baltimore 2011

Fog

Gorgeous Stag

To Denise. To Y.

animal and machine

mutations and pleasures

Johan Jönson

2

Two black swans cook all morning in the kitchen, making Red Pringles and Alone-and-Coatless Pringles and Pringles of Seesaw, of Jungle Gym, setting the silver pond with Pringle Bowls and Pringle Juice and napkins for Pringle dabbing. Ronald Reagan arrives for lunch. He sits in the best chair and it collapses so he unfolds himself up like a mechanical shadow and sits in the second best chair. The swans silently serve the Pringles. Ronald Reagan says, "What manner of lunch is this!?" Reagan's words sound like hard dry black meat. The birds cannot comprehend; never has a house guest refused the Pringles. Flustered, they sing, "These are Pringles pick up two Pringles put one upside down on the other now hold the Pringles to your lips and we can all speak song together." The sky tilts hammer/tong. The second best chair collapses and the front leg gashes open Ronald Reagan's shin. He sits there bleeding, from shrapnel, from a war on the imagination. He is so hungry, so angry now; the only way to save face is to destroy the birdhouse entire. Do you understand? Are you still fighting the good fight? Possibly not; on the wrong side sleepless, legs flailing out. Your soul a black feather, a coiling rent feather, a question mark of blood.

[the rain at this time heavy enough to appear as smoke on the streets. paper strips peeled and fluttered from the many billboards. some children mistook them for leaves]

1

Earth Observation Satellite

Doubt arrived, you know, Doubt, the common doom. When the Ones gathered, the Zeros would leave town for the moonshine springs below the lake. When the Zeros met, the Ones would go to their basements and shoot crossbows into the unfinished walls—pock, pock, pock. So the town felt drenched, wormed, blistered, floated. The stores would not store. The asphalt ribbons curled themselves into loops and went rolling into the sky. The rivers lay still, and slept. So thank gods for country music. Country music solved everything. That and the plastic provided by Andy Warhol. (All of this altered my life profoundly; I would eventually learn to drink whiskey from a kidney bean can, and to cry.) The stores refilled with plastic. The Ones and Zeros went forth and multiplied. There is a plaque in the town: ANDY WARHOL AND COUNTRY MUSIC SAVED US. WE WANT TO BE PLASTIC. WE WANT TO LIE DOWN NOW. TO DIE NOW. TO WAKE UP TOMORROW AT THE MALL.

on a banana seat bicycle
a man in beads
a bobcat vest says,
"The golden arches—
it's cleavage"

[to live outside the law you must be _____]

A Celebrity Pens a Letter Concerning "Monogram" by Robert Rauschenberg

a tire stick on a goat i have seen goats do worst things we own goats so i can answer this one easy a goat always to go up higher goat always to stand on cars and hey bails the well and one we found on the roof it clumb up the truck bed the cab jump the house roof we could not get goat down so grandpa shot it rifle down we cooked it hole in the ground like mexicans do that was first time i seen my grandpa fall he fell yes no he fall yes after shot the goat fell to his knees it scared me OK

9 items noted on gravely shoreline:

1. water snake, striped brown and tan
2. sunglasses sans one lens
3. husk of cluster bomblet
4. blue flip flop (bottle opener ingeniously embedded in heel)
5. eroded boulder, creamy, perfectly round. face like a clouded crystal ball
6. empty wine bottle
7. sex
8. punctured crow
9. plastic rose

Observed on Tuesdays

Yes, I have seen the lock of glide from the deer. Like empty space. Like a dream. It made no sound, and then right there, upon you. It ached for hobbling. I have seen the wrappings, of aluminum flower stems, some form of Holiday. Some form of metallic leaves, of capillary. The Sunday of Highly Polished, of Fabric Evaporate. The Tuesday of Copper Thorns. Etc. On their long necks, like that painter. (I do not recall—many, many days of holding my breath.) Yes, I have seen the rivers dammed, blockades of extended palms, whispers past your head (phosphorus or maybe stone skips), so our bodies are filled with water now, the Laboratory Seven say, and that makes sense: you cannot stop a river. We move from place to place. The sun shot out the throat of the earth. The moon all hubcapped beneath the sea. Around the base of a ragged bush, I hid. I lived on the latest Potato Flavor: Fog Gorgeous Stag. One old deer toppled off a billboard. To the highway. To the creek—its red blood off red clay, off sunglasses and a cane, off flowers; in the sunglass reflection, a wonderful thing: single white wild blossom. Now you don't believe me. I see it in your sighs. I was the same way. "Just like a movie," I mumbled. But it was not. It was a photo of a movie, a painting of the photo, and then someone set a fitful dance to the image, or…Fold. Unfold. Fold. I cannot say. There is litigation, and listen to the scrawled letter of my shower drip (again). Time for the deep tub. I will try. I will let my breath hold me. Will let anything bloom. Where did my glad go? Fold. Unfold. Fold. Modigliani. Sure, OK.

[fold like a coat thrown to the floor. unfold like picked cattails
or the tots of tater

overcooked/exploded]

Square 11

—The air and water, the see/feel/smell/taste, all percussive—inside, outside the body—walked and walked of: that is fog.

—Suburbs.

—I.D.

—The day you told me to proof myself. To document.

— Air, not as flown or fell, not as swirled in, moved about—but as breathed. Seized by the lungful (above trampled fog as box.). The scuffed bolt of Frankenstein's neck, stapling the carotid.

—Choose: PURITY or DANGER.

—To devote several sentences to morning I chose incorrect profession. Morning I wed in a church although my body camouflage, a Home/Garden/Patio Show, the stained glass all telegraph, as in cluster fuck/bomb. Morning I roped home the dog that ingests underpinnings of my push-back, of my hope.

—Excuse me.

—Screen as dumpster.

—Ultimate machines.

—Add three ice cubes.

—Make stand bold.

—A form to fill (in/out).

—Blood as salt. The framed shoulder area of an ambulance driver's coat. IV bags, when bloated/full or stepped upon/empty.

—The first to form tuxedos from thunderclap—that is we. Bowties of binoculars. We built the fucking displays. And we got paid. Hard. Villas and apartments around the world—all square. High Living. High Living. Is that all? You bet your sweet ass.

Your garbage. Your garbage bin.

[get your finger out your mouth]

—Coffers, foreign envelopes, medical tents, trenches, dice, chest,

chest wounds, commands, tumblers, torture rooms, sugar

cubes, world views, fuck yous.

—Any half life.

—Any hour you half life.

—Any hour we meet and square off.

—Any positive reinforcement.

—Any shredded metal (see the collecting flies?).

hum

[my skull a circle. my heart a circle

mouth a circle

O]

Transcript

Found: Confrontation. Yes, I was responsible, but it was likewise a common act. A war dance, I suppose. They taught me to be absolutely still until God rang the bell.

My life at that time a triangle—air, food, water—and, like a triangle of razor blades, required no sharpening.

I will not discuss the cage. My little bent reflection in the bars. I was told the bars were actually glazed clay, and hollow, filled with the ashes of every participant before me.

Tuesdays were the best, my day off. God would bring a thin broth of alphabet soup (maybe three letters, tops). She would sing and play (on synthesizer) one of the fourteen Good Songs.

I had to keep three razor blades in my mouth during every Confrontation, the entire time. Can you imagine?

People say that, but I never felt warm.

Yes, I met him and her.

I had this thing where halogen lamps were actually eyes. Or maybe stars. I had this way of telling myself the Universe still heard my thrumming.

May I drink from your aluminum packet?

Oh, about chapels of steel and glass monasteries. One was this set of earphones made of hollow stone. She sang one song about a tanning salon out by the firing range. I'm not sure why I remember only those three, I just do.

Today? That's easy: sleep. Because I have to ask, is now a nightmare from which I will indeed wake, or was it then?

Yes.

No.

I wouldn't. But that is up to you.

[a cell phone fits the Victorian
watch pocket. it is warm]

Spoons

—You are suffocating me. I like it.

—Early April, the nests of breeding bluebirds.

—The ill-invented spoon. Oh, I could go on…lung to lunge. Look, I refuse to lie to you. I'm so ill of my inspirations.

—You have a masseuse. I have masturbation. We have a dish on our roof, but so?

—A seashell works perfectly fine.

[*well, your hand was blown off*
so they filled your glove
with rolled cotton]

—Henry Ford tumbling out of a canoe and drowning. You can peer down and see him, the flowing water morphing his face, blurring his pink hands. His expression resembles an asphalt floor. He is pinned by the wonderful roots of a tree (trees as correct, the truest occupants of the earth). Look, his vest is finally fluttering. Unbutton one, unbutton two. His tie is a flapping tongue. His shoes just zipped away like blondness and bright eyes. Up floats four wine corks and two socks all humping. Up floats a white cough of porcelain. Up floats two hundred and fourteen million musty dollar bills. Bubbles out his mouth, bubbles laughing. Up floats a radio. Minutes pass, somewhere up high a woodpecker caws, a bee bumbles by, and even now the bubbles are whisked away, and so many wooden spoons. Must have had pocketfuls of pilfered wooden spoons, down-way, over/under current, riffles and raff, palmed in eddies, kissed goodbye—all the spinning wooden spoons!

spoon for balancing eggs

cocaine spoon

coffee spoon

spoon of drawer, its place: return, return

spoon for administering (other obscure info)

spoon of dark patch around the eye

tongue spoon

silver spoon

sleeping bag opiate cuddle spoon (peak)

tumor spoon

cozy-in-the-bathtub spoon

death/loss/love spoon

boot spoon

ear spoon

absinthe spoon

spoon of bra

spoon of arcing shells

                              [red
                              and phosphorus
                              and]

rattail spoon

spoon-stuck-in-throat-of-fish

apostle spoon

baby spoon

spoon that supports and feeds evasion

chowder spoon

horn spoon

spoon of, the cup of my synapse (this is where the long hair of my mistakes fill bucket

after bucket. i want to say hotel. all I have draped there)

naked spoon

grenade spoon

prison escape spoon

sugar tong

                              [basically the day i wore
                              your underwear to my job
                              as a therapist. it was
                              a moist day
                              and a little fog rolled off the lake]

mind-bent spoon

ladle

spork

Six Lies

Thunder during snow. Disintegration. A runover snake in the road leading to the Night Dance. Josephine Baker tumbles off a roof. This moon low and large. How often will we misspell names? Josephine Baker bruised and corrosive, is that the opinion? We've had drought forever and people keep talking drought. Someone better, better do something soon, but no one does a thing. THE PLAN IS TO LOVE YOUR LONELINESS. Josephine Baker's fractured heel on the baked dirt. Her dress riding up her knees. The top buttons flung away. Lines of sweat along her shoulder blades. A whit, a whit of difference—explain to us. Josephine Baker flashes some triangle of breast, thick hard nipple. They won't give morphine for the pain; they suspect alcohol. They are well-fed. Examine the facts at hand: 1) Every mailbox cut open. 2) The use of service elevators. 3) A snarl at the door. There is something sheen/sweet/hard about flesh, you whisper. Listen to me: there is no plan. We should be ashamed.

The Liar's Meal
The Whopper
The Coldest Beer on Earth
I Do Drops
Hot Saliva

[…as implicated by his top hat and green shirt—just a sliver, see it?—resting on his stool, is seen in a sort of aesthetic tussle, unknowing of the prophetic butterfly outside his window, a lateral view…]

[This is not dress rehearsal
Check]

Instructions Posted on Aging

1. Obtain your largest candy cane.

2. Hollow out the core of your largest candy cane.

3. Fill the candy cane core with broken teeth of glass.

4. Hold this device to your dominant eye. (There is a method involving triangles and mirrors for identifying your dominant eye.)

5. Use this device for struggling uphill. For releasing dogs from any type of trap. For cracking open cans of soda wine. For Not Saying Another Word. For unhinging the hidden door. For holding up the sky. For wiping the shine of sweat. For oiling or combing or detangling hair. For deputation. For observing bluebirds. For watching your own back.

Snakes

—A husband's footprints.

—Moments in comfortable chairs. Moments waiting for the universe.

—The border of a country.

—Holy shit!

—Would you like to have coffee with me?
—I would rather decompose than have cof-
fee with you.

—Most any seizure.

—Lips (the spaces between).

—Contrails.

a celebrity pens a letter concerning snakes:

[snakes will hung in trees or shoe closets i know most shacks hold a snake corn cribs a barn to but snakes dont get up drink milk from cows teat thats a lie snakes can wind that wire like that other go when early cold look for cricks and sun like tin metel will move slow my sun day was when we came canoe round the ox bend and hit the bush their snake fell in boat i know sara can holler sound like broken gate or stuck rabbits or snare one i pin the snake with that paddle flipped over the water clar we looked it swim way a big S a runover snake will crawl one day

bite for two people will try to swurv to hit
the snake i guess i know the time i shoot the
snake OK granpa said why did you just saw
the snake a big black one S in the dust shade
simmons trees and brain slow fast that heart
did that and knees felt fell off cherry piker
sort of OK and i just got hurry OK and shot
the snake grandpa scalwed me then grandpa
said a snake done nothing if you feel to hurt
hurt quick why don't you think that snake is
forever now off the earth and what have you
done good OK i said grandpa what the bible
say one snake aint all snakes one thing aint
ever thing he said did you even have a bad
dog i course laughed gus was the worse dog
gus dug al the pigs free and ate the pigs gus
ripped mee maw's shirts form the line gus ate
my sunday bass whole gus ate the roof tar
barells gus ran up under grandpa truck two
times and second time dead you even had a
good dog grandpa said dont you know chip
was the one who follow me to school show
up after lunch after i got the bus chip walk
the highway and my class that day my room
so far and all laughing likeing me now oh
chip i lamint chip and that the best dog easy
so what you know of dogs now grandpa said
snakes will lay down railroad tracks to soak
up the silver i seen a snake eat a snake like
a circl there but them circlss cant go rolling

down a road thats a lie most times people
see a cottonmouth it ain't but a water snake
people like to say they seen a cottonmouth
i dont stand why people just like to say big
things grandpa said what you shoud do is
learn a snake i mean sit and still and look
on the water a big silent S listen to it on the
water OK]

—I like to hide curled in closets during parties.

And a Little
Horse-loving Girl

Rubber hatchets. Corn cob pipes. Fried Pepsi. Fried ears of corn. A laser that will etch your own face onto the handle of a lint remover ($8).

[the weather at this point is partly cloudy. you can imagine blue jeans or:

....
....
...   ]

A spiraling ramp.

One young lady with sharp hipbones and a pelvis made for sunlight. Actual paper fans! Is that a large Indian?

Shhh…

An Armani suit that looks perfectly worn but is perfectly new. Teeth. Microphones in a bouquet of clown noses.

Is this on? John Wayne came off the mountain. Or should I say, *The hero came off the mountain*, but I don't need to, not now, or even this evening over cocoa at the tavern of Free Talk. (Will you wear the sleeveless series of coils?) He staggered, he did so. You people don't know staggering. He staggered out the trailer and threw up, thrice. That was earlier, with the orange slices. Wait. It was the sun all crazy marching and kicking up the sky tumbling into a cloud-meadow or should I say papier-mâché meteor then lower, smaller, a basketball careening away—crag, cliff, scree, avalanche!—a dimpled orange nuzzling the crease of his open hand. It felt cool there, solid and real. This may have been mystical, or altitude illness (his left shin confirmed as bruised). He unraveled a head bandage and flung it near someone, this I know. Moist with perspiration, his essence, not something easily abandoned, but… He said, "Heal yourself." Or maybe *deal or feel*, not so important, his actual words. What is then? First, turning back would result in further misery and death. That's just physics. Second, now you see why everything shone in his bomber jacket. The first-aid kit, the yellow phone. And all these oranges. Finally, I know you want him to apologize. So, OK, the man apologizes. Here: *He is sorry you misunderstand him.*

This is Literally All the Info I Have at the Moment

We came across a sign on which DRUGGED had been painted in crude brush-strokes. There were two of us left, and L opened the sign with some form of lubricated saw. Out fell a blue key. We walked for miles. (I won't say how far. Impossible now to revisit those footsteps—their odd, alluring rhythm. It took me so long to… well. I know those foot-rises/footfalls were everything. Or let me quote L: "This type of walking worries. I have moments I prefer it to the light, to the water or the very air we breathe.") L would leave the path, to stagger off into shafts of shadow. Would complain of irritability. Would demand we stop. Why? To install a window in a nearby tree. To vacuum up the snow. (L insisted we were suffocating in snow; simply not true.) To set up a field kitchen or dig a slate-lined vat. I said no. We instead stopped by a tumbling stream for a light meal of yogurt cups. Then discovered the cavern.

Lady Day falls from a door in the ceiling.

Lady Day wipes off her knees, clears her throat, rearranges a wilted gardenia pinned to her hair.

Lady Day sighs. We inhale, and finally sleep.

(*You didn't even use the key!*

Oh you. Still not listening.)

[blue]

One Mythology

In the year of Thud, of McEclipse, during the Third Purge of Knees, to own a single word of writing—a dot of black on white—was to symbolize, to say *I am this*, tick tock and venomous and verve, an endangered thing in a forest falling, wonderful and wrecked. On an island, in a cave, hidden from all seekers; and they say she owned a book! They found her with shreds of binding, a residue of glue… Can you imagine, can you witness now? *Where walk the fucking pages!* A howl of fog light, of shrieking blade. *Tell us straight away!* They say she was laughing. They say they found not a single word. She read them all, pried them from the page with her skillful fingers; folded them into intricate shapes. They say her name was your name, and she lifted the letters into the sky. This is how we have birds.

Methods

1. Why not just eat a steak?

2. It seems the ordeal will never end.

3. Lights on.

4. Stocking-footed.

5. Longed, one day (not who I was).

6. Move. But stay low.

7. Under the mattress.

8. Must we throw flames?

9. *Settle.*

10. Voices fog-off/lift volume through generations. (Do you ever shriek/scald at mirrors, madam normal?)

11. Tip: A male condom and a female condom will cancel out one another.

12. Sleep.

13. And, you know, you fuck on the foreheads of clouds and it rains.

[-I don't have anything
-You don't need it]

14. Pepper grinder limbs. Breasts like Socrates.

15. Ignitable putty.

16. My breath is rotten, yours thin.

17. The dance of blood-n-guts, of ear-buds and $10,000 ice sculptures, cloud to cloud to cloud—clearly drunk out of our minds.

18. I should read more books.

19. And this is we?

20. What is the Internet?

21. You furl up your flower. You hide it inside a box of kitchen matches.

22. Like when she let loose the lead balloons. (They smothered the land.)

23. Like two slabs of bacon.

24. Like 5 friends (the most ever really).

25. Like what you hide profound, some crevice.

26. Velvet—you know what I mean.

27. Like the Family Weekend Golf Outing.

[the world a taffy machine, cranking out Tom Cruise and quivering knees. Tom buys a maul. a pike and hammer. Tom goes all teenager on the clouds. he lops the heads off the rivers. he mows the grass and mows the stars and mows to sleep the beauty. no more bubbling foam or giant water lilies or oranges spilling crazily onto the floor. this Tom Cruise, he's a landfill to his own self. he's a savior, etc. there glows a grass so green i sigh suspicious. we have questions, sir. we are preparing a memo. where is the bird going to perch now?]

28. Like frigates, fleas, goldfish crackers.

29. What folly!

30. Shhhhhhh

31. People flow in opposite directions.

32. Fake hallway conversations.

33. Hoof-beats, a snow of plucked insect wings. Almost beautiful. (The rain curled into a ball. We slipped beneath the chasses, into mascaras of mud.)

34. (With all this. Now. My largest regret is all the people I did not…)

35. Like coiled black wire.

36. Like coiled black wire.

37. Like clatter.

38. Like the emptiness which squelches me, the laniary due retentions of this knife. What knife? Beyond today, as far as one can see, are the friends (I said 5, it's 3), the un-heard yelps of the countryside. Above us, low sky, a little sad, as in cloudy. Once in a while the sun speaks, vague as a frown. Or.

39. People still lick the intelligent pig?

40. Do they know me?

41. The nastiest, biggest spider I ever fucking saw!

42. My day.

43. Like coiled things.

44. Don't ask me to explain.

45. Where in the hell am I?

46. Like coiled-up bluebirds, splayed out utensil (the cup of their wings, swirl of wind, the ruffling feathers; the telephone line shadows on their stiffening gaze). I stumbled upon a wet pile of bluebirds, all of them executed, no meat taken, their mouths frozen open, their tiny pink tongues, their yellow eyes staring in dull amazement—that did it for me.

too bad

too bad

[and Tom Cruise says, anyone want to make out? i'm bored]

Code (Interrupted in Transit)

Mary 9

No one cares about the fish. They are not cute. They fly invisible beneath the sea. Dependence for vain now. This business quickly over. If you would be so kind. Castle the library. Castle with the body. Castle with the sea. I 216.9.29'd, a 158.8.15. without .74.9.32. The early, squirrely clouds have come from the chicken-wire sky leaving only cages of shade to overlay a painted-on-cardboard lumber espresso. The name of your dog. Spray down the attic, Mary 9. Waver in the west. Extend the middle finger. Do not bring your hawk. The giggle of a three-legged frog. It makes me dizzy. It makes me dizzy. Where do you want to die today? One hour delay. Listen. I have the pleasure of 294.9.18. 19.8.36. Possibly of the serious light. Tuck the final moments under your arm like a fattened goose. We will swing on strings. Listen. We draw no iron. These fish move faster than Porsches. You will have no doubt heard by now. The chair is indeed against the wall.

[294.9.141414---]

Day 8

Why must you hold a weapon? Why do you press lips to its steel? Why do you mumble love? Why did you smear it all, the red, the blue, the green? Who swallows the wishbone? You come so seldom. You follow some clumsy procedure. Why did you roll the heavy stone? You were seen placing spider webs. You were *witnessed*, drawing a chalk line, shoving the meek across…

> (Here we have an image of a demonstration/doorway
>
> of a thin white Kleenex fluttering with broken wing
>
> of sodden, felled animal crackers.)

Why did you abandon your friend in his time of need? Why did you grab her hand, to let it go? Collect all the crumbs of sandwich bread and such, is that your method? Crumbs and wind, crumbs cast into the wind. Why did you drink the Clorox Sunshine Bleach, and wait for *us* to die? You better keep one eye open (though this isn't about you). Look, there goes Albert Einstein, on the wonderfully large unicycle of his own devising. He's pedaling home, but there is no home. Only flame.

Come for a Day
Stay for a Life

I remember hands melting
(or I mean swept out of other hands.)

—10,000 tattoos on my forehead. How am I going to hide my forehead?

—And you say I have an easy, shiftless look.

—The river is this way.
  The river I am.
  Now: steeped.

—We are running out of time.

—Choose: HEALTHY or UNHEALTHY.

—Tit for Tat, they call it—this before the eardrums. Before everything was blue screen and surrounding roar of engines. Lonely, lonely we, a half moon of furniture, each slurping our own hollow chests, our glowing digits.

—Oh, it *is* in writing. How is that working out for you? How is anything working out?

—Glimpse.

—40,000 tons of signs. Their voice the yellow of well-oiled smoke rings, of cooked words. Glaring everywhere, tacked to automobile hides, hung from windmill forests, glued to the walls of glaciers. In the screech of a pressed cricket: SOMEONE NOW REPORT HER! Then in smaller mumble: SHE WAS SAW DRINKING RIVER. SHE WAS SAW EATING MUD. Then in the tiniest red, dried and flaked whisper: WALK OUR EYES TO HER HIDING. An image of a flaming wheelbarrow. I'll be the first to admit we did nothing. Those days I spent collecting grapevine. I had a serious habit at the time. Sometimes you sit there. You look straight up, and you see the moon—hushed eye, bright and smooth, carving headlamp—and you're captivated, washed over slant-ways, oblivious to your situation: that you kneel at the bottom of a well. Alfred Hitchcock awoke on a gauzy Thursday. His bedsprings shrieked as he exited the room. He filmed the signs, every one. He did the rack-focus, the salt dissolve. He entered our homes and showed the films. How we stumbled through the streets of wilderness then; how we flailed our echoing limbs! Gnashing every sign down.

a celebrity pens a letter concerning yellow:

[tail of a bluegill bream cook them over fire potatoe chips OK can throw hoppers ticks on water and come up circles makes a bap sound we call it bapping whittail antler shed squirrels fall but find easy if you get early look clost bottoms of grandpas feet mee maws hands shake like the sky this man painted i remember the highway said they buy so much maws land for the Dysberg out there airport needed dirt make her pretty pond she said go strait to hell they just come back grandpa said they had domane they never built that pond none felled persimmon get stitches and put the prsimon on the end whip way high for fun sara and me done that for hours skull of small raccoon cap to miller beer few minutes fore tornado sky like bar soap my mee maw said tornaddos followed her all over the county no matter where she hid a silo in the gulley in a broken dishwashing under a pond stepped on turtle back grandpa says the older you get the more big ones you tell cause no one will listen a sleeve of sara's summertime dress it fell and i picked a toadstool on cow pie little speckles you eat that toadstool you will fly three days up high then fall strait down on the road and die bruise my ma bruise my father i will not say here even my grandpa says questions you do not anser even to a teacher or a preacher or a god]

I know I met a small girl
and I lay my head on a wooden table
and I trouble-dreamt
and she was gone

The Odor of Thin Cigars

Iggy Pop shooting the breeze. Machine the breeze. Iggy Pop with a fresh bob haircut (made of flour, water, food coloring). Everything ferments (like sky), so everyone intoxicated (like sky). The foaming sky. The arterial breeze. Iggy Pop, in a husky voice: "The morning is a motherfucker!" Censor that. The morning is a white husky dog in Scrub Land with a target arrow in its side, curling microphone cord of blood, tongue out and asking—who did this, to me? (I am a white husky dog. I am topography.)

"…all of this made by people."

"Are you real?"

"A few years pass."

Large, lonely Machine. The breeze. Yes, the Trials of Knees. Here's the thing: I still do enjoy balloons. And Iggy Pop says not to feed the trees. Do not cut or wheedle. Do not look at limbs. Climb them!

"The system can't handle this," said she.

Crack.

[the journalists asleep in their hotels. some entwined. most with hangovers. their entire lives suddenly a difficult physics equation—something they have no ability to solve. a young girl (the she above) films everything with a head-cam. the recording receives more Vid-Hits than shark attacks, though less than dogs being struck by troop carriers]

Whenever it Rains

1. Nothing.
2. Condensation pimpling the skin of grenade.
3. Muffle.
4. Nothing. Then:

Tuesday on the floor. (I have the last brass mail slot in the world.) On the front of the postcard was an image of a man with umbrella walking under scaffolding. It read: "You descend, they follow. I suppose it's a parlor game. I don't say herding if I lead, but let's not. There was a man known for biting diamonds. They had a book could decipher the odors in any dream. Also an ape we fed, until one day we looked closer and the ape was a potted tree with limbs of holiday lights. YOU MAY ONLY ATTEND THE FAIR ON MONDAYS, TUESDAYS, THURSDAYS, FRIDAYS, AND WEEKENDS. I just had an urge to gusto laugh, but I don't love you (not really) so will instead strike a ball with a mallet, though I have no mallet or ball. I will make the motion, in the air. Last night I entered the beige tent and slept with _____. And then _____. And then _____. Three times, before I even tasted glue. At the gift shop's gift shop. Downstairs, on the roof. 'How are things?' 'Things are fine.' And the safe will yawn open. Grab the jewels (kind of the point of opening the safe, yes?). Fine, I feel fine. Fine, I feel fine. Fine, I feel…WEDNESDAYS WE WOULD PREFER YOU SLEEP PROFOUNDLY. This one morning I startle up pecking like a Cornish hen and this big funk-cloud of mildewed grain, and you know why? I am a Cornish hen."

[i took this dispatch and ground it into sand-
like dots and filled an hour glass with words]

The Infinite Social Life
of a Thing

Say the reign of the stones. Hail stones walloped windows. Limestones flattened chrome. Say soapstones scrubbed the land of doors: screen, French, oven. (Nefertiti dialing phone psychics.) Sandstones brushed away the crazily stretched metal the camera flash bulbs the silver cufflinks the pearl oysters the black helicopter blades the etc. Say the sculptures of _____ erased by Alabaster. (Adonis splitting Paxil tablets.) Marbles, giant marbles—or call it what you will, flaming eyes, space stones—screeching from the sky, into all the lakes, the swimming pools; ruptured all the yolks and deep the water swirls down the drains. Storms of granite, thunderstorms of granite, the rain of stone.

Bull's-eye!

Singeing heart!

Every mirror!

(Cleopatra staggering in galoshes through the streets of acne…window frames of smiling faces.)

God

[Oprah, do you remember when you rescued the child from his life of raising sheep? when you snatched his overalls and ceased his convulsions on stage? you gave him a silver mouth mask. he is now a keypunch operator, also horny, happy, handsome, free]

Gorgeous are the chemists. The crystallized trees, the way they scrub the sky. The way the snowflakes stagger. (I smell ozone, almonds, then nothing. Fingers numb-out, turn blue. My lips grow thick.) But thanks for reattaching us to the earth. For setting all the pigs aflame. Gorgeous are the Neat, the Clean, the Artists who draw the protesters. The suck of satellites. Those who suck the satellites (example, me). What is your nature? Stupefied stones licking themselves. Open mouths of rivers. Gorgeous their words, like PINK ALERT or BEWARE THE LOVE OF STRANGE ONES. Madness now illegal. Dizziness and clutch, illegal. Seizing fragments of the Universe, illegal. Also please cease lifting your hands into bits of sky, any type of signaling. Gorgeous the Law. Downhill running, tumbling, very long leg rubbing; reading of footprints; cooking on quiet fires; rolling leaves into cylinders between thumb and finger; speculating breathlessly—all illegal. Hail the category! (I said do not lift your hand, and then you just went and...) Hail the Overall Function! Gorgeous were the clouds? We do not deny. But that was then, and this, as is clear, is *now*.

—God's favorite song: the vaccination song.

—The status of God's memory: flotsam, partly flotsam, inhaled completely, clear.

—God's preferred weather: oh, cold rainfalls, a type of nubbled hail.

—What God doodles: coughing one hundred dollar bills.

God [2]

It was Her habit to drive over to the open-air café in the early evening, and there, as I have said, She would drink, She would talk, She would look at Her Favorite Thing, a blue rag with a Kool-Aid stain. "This is not Kool-Aid," She would tell most anyone. "This is not a rag. This is a piece of Bonnie Parker's dress, soaked in her very own blood. It is worth more than all the wars of freedom or 460 prayers concerning enemies, butter, or dust." Three types of people frequented the open-air café: those who routinely cut their lawn, those who never cut their lawn, and those woebegone souls who dreamed of one day owning a lawn—green and vast, lush as a secret handshake, as low flames burning atop a lake along a back road—of weighing that significant question: *to cut, or not to cut*. I forgot to mention the winter garden and the duck. The duck would stand in the winter garden outside the café and talk in higher math; it would say, "Zero, twelve, twenty-three, one-hundred-and-sixty-four." Or: How many men Bonnie murdered. How many Clyde shot down (most with backs turned). The age of Bonnie Parker. The number of bullets they fired into the chest pocket of her dress.

[fairness lurches

laughs across

the countryside]

Symptoms

Skulk the city in your thin soles, the populous line the streets, the populous turn their backs. You are stuffed ass-ward into garbage cans. A young woman sprinkles indigo into your scalp. Locked into cages of shoulder pads. The odor of sweat. Someone scorches cloves/cuticles/claw-curls into the skin of your sleeping rags. You begin a thought of tattoo removal. You possibly dream. Two worms wriggle prematurely across your back.

Photophobia. Or February as sister.

Sobbing.

A desire to gnaw the gumballs rattling your skull.

2000 fake vodkas. Shadow puppets.

> [enlarged
> heart
> as reliable bomb]

Home is calling.

Your stomach holy. Your heart clotted in its own string. Islands of kidneys shrapnel/ splayed, in unnecessary battle, an unnecessary campaign. (People do die.) The ear-saddles mounted on kneeling horses, jagged curtsies. Your chin as jetty. Forehead as experimental airplane. Drink, drink, Fool. Feller of false stories. Drink. Plummet now. Anything you enjoy—cease. Or hide every wackjob (keen word), every knee-knock.

Inability to read.

Inability to disinfect your headset.

> [you will no longer use the yo-yo. why? it will weaken the string. the string is weakened, then what? you will no longer use the yo-yo]

A substance behind your kneecaps, an excellent jelly.

Your special rags are suddenly "just a bunch of leaves, really." A tendency to murmur.

Widespread aches and pains.

A trifle pretentious. Like maybe your fingers are growing larger, going cartoon, maybe you see them pan-caking like airships above you.

Diarrhea.

A desire to claim.

A desire to remember a thing.

Additional killing of hawks.

Several Useful Prayers

—Prayer of I am water.

—Prayer of always moving.

> [this quirk where she pours warm wine into her mouth—this while showering—and will gurgle a song and ask her husband (he'll be flossing) to name the song. he never gets the song and it makes her glint even more alone, like in here (jabs chest with finger). she lifts weights, too, while in the shower, one arm at a time, these dumb-bells, 7 ½ pounds. thinking of ways to do four things simultane-ously: play gurgle-song game, intoxicate awful brain, lift weights, cleanse body. it seems galactic. she figures she will live 150 years]

—Prayer of endless white hallways

    endlessly dirtied

    endlessly scrubbed.

> [there goes an elbow, a giggling lobe of liver]

> [what posture! what a voice! you should be a credit card or snowfall]

—Prayer of fashionable yellow goggles. Camera quills. Prayer of tethered birds. Silver bells and tassels. The sky filled with ropes and trembling chips of flint. The sky filled with cawing. You call this sport? (I push and I push and I push...) Prayer of something left, cold and dark, forgotten cups of tea, closed fingers (a morbid horror of planting grapes, and no real hope of wine). Now my heart falls gun-shot, all crabbed, snarly, and stupid. Prayer for 7 ½ seconds. Prayer for words to revisit the throat, the hole filled, the silver hearse without any wheel at all. (It is with real sadness…) I might as well look into my chilly broth and see a dog. Or my telephone is now an apartment building and I sleep on the worried brow of Button 9. Operator? Things are wrong. Things are wrong. Prayer of sun (even if raging). Prayer of light. You must paint your eyes. Then scrape away.

—Prayer of viscosity. (Why must things slow as they accumulate?)

—of weaving.

—of lost convoys lumbering in the night.

—of my arms in a basket, my bleeding shins, and two eyeballs rolling about like brothers in brand new clothes: this is my body.

[listen: we are basically produce, a bag of produce—open us to sweet air, and we will soon melt

or murk]

[listen: the word is hot

don't touch]

—*Amen*

Prayer of Gun Ownership

a celebrity pens a letter concerning grease:

[i guess i was 12 my first remington said the little book their to clan the gun that the gun was packed in shippin grease and oil clean it good fore you go shoot thangs i took it to grandpa and says grandpa how to do this i don't know much i am 12 and he put his cigar down my remington walked outside shot it right up the air i mean both barells loud handed it to my hands said boy that's how you clan a damn shotgun]

—A person sucks the steel. A person likes the taste.

—A person shoots an aspirin out of the air.

—A person crumples. A child says it felt like a stinging bee and that a fox lives in the neighborhood, an actual fox. (The fox is a pet of God.)

Click.

Click.

—Don't.

Click.

—Do not shoot me.

Please?

Additional Prayer (with List of Potential Summer Employment)

A skeleton rimmed in gold walks proudly down the avenue, waving (to you, to me), waving into the gangly limbs, the spangly limbs, the glass windows and smiles of Marilyn Monroe's face. [Prayer of everything that eludes.] Her whole body dash and comma. She keeps pausing to kiss things. Hey now! Stop. How would you like to buy a silver lair? Marilyn Monroe grips you by the apostrophe and screams, "Look at me wriggle, look at me wriggle—I wish you all were so moved you would set me free!"

1. Shaver of Pencils
2. Gut Piler
3. Heart Cupper
4. Huncher of Gray Knots
5. Striker
6. Lifeguard
7. Mint Thinner
8. Happy Person Nearby Famous Person
9. Mule

After Doing Smiles

I jump now at the slap of light. At the kick and silences of glistening (as in words). At my name. She gave up too. Pause. I will not talk paper. If I talk paper I will mumble limbs and limbs crack/crumble/fall into a thousand breaths—there is bound (bind, binding, binder full of albino wolves) to be swaying. I said pause. Her skin was leathery. No. I said no. I would like a sandwich so big tasting like frothy cardboard/leak of light and a need to drag it home (but will not, full and disgusted). Did I do that? Six leftovers: 1: Drooling a snagged relationship back onto the field. 2: Letting the hawks curdle and spoil. 3: Bottled warfare. 4: Kid's Meal of Cowardly _____. 5: Why must someone wake me? Why not wake myself? 6: You left The Crucible on. How many times have I said, Please turn off The Crucible? How do I know I still exist? Slap of light. Laughter, photographs. Muffled lens of chortle. (As always, God has thrown Her body down onto the sand. Yes, She is making love with a young man while addressing Her audience.) Click. Click. Click. "These seem too glossy," I say. She snorts and leaps back. "Too glossy! Want me to take them again?"

[in several images i get my ass
kicked. i.e.:

oh never mind]

a celebrity pens a letter concerning mona lisa:

[you trying to make me lamint i guess didn't
think art means much like grandpa said one time

art is a rich persons nap and working person
don't get no nap never but I know that smile
now like with the crick out back by the prop-
erty line i crick can make you feel things fishin
or wading sometimes be in near water there
makes some way inside and always know you
told us first day what is the price of a sunrise
what is the price of ocean something and know
why does grandpa go down the crick and wade
down all day i seen that smile and now that
smile is wash away]

sneezes of blood

Transcript [2]

That you gave me, the green drink. It made me think, "When the tangled pages of snow bounce off the tree fingers, a small bird, a light coma of bones, size of an ancient bell, sometimes stumbled, fell to its knees/flung to the earth, yaw and staple, sometimes stuck out its tongue and licked the crust."

Don't blame the bird.

I am giving one example. We have our own science. They detect movement. So stay still, you can jot that down.

[obedience: born into a grave]

They might collect from miles…a cough, a kind word, or the milking of an itch. Windmill air across the earth. Then process: hair, tentacles, corn chip belch, plastic disc, three keys, the salt of your eyes.

That is true. The bird had an icon around its neck.

The night was blustery, cold, disruptively so—off went the bird.

The slogans were WELL SWELL and WORTH BLIGHT and RING CHAINS. Times I longed to write the slogans. I appreciate the throat of language.

LOSE BALANCE. GOOD MOTHER. ABANDON EYE. STATIC BRING. LAY LOWER. MARSH SOON. TAKE TECH. LIGHT YOUR WATER. TIME IS NIGHT. SINGLE DIAL. SMOKE A JOKE. RETAIN SICK. SMART OVER. KIND OFF MAN. SAVE WAVES. FANGLE YOUR NEIGHBOR. LOVE THE FAIR. ANTHOLOGIZE.

A half-pecked photo. So? A glob of spittle in a glass tube. Are you implying? Good thick gloves that somewhat resemble, I suppose, when drying on a stick by the fire.

I don't know. Why ask me? I have resisted my entire path in life.

That you gave me, the green drink. So I think, "We struggle for life on the hilltops and stick out our arms and wait..."

Somewhere or someone. Look at us.

In our hearts the quiet of a hospital room

of mirrors

of keeping yourself together.

When?

Today.

> [one minute I'm here
>
> next minute I'm gone
>
> that's me]

The last time you saw a bluebird on its knees?

We Lie in Any Stream

We are wandering the forest. Not so easy to run from the sweet sounds of Good Brain (Why not towards them?). The Hunting Horns angular and logical as elbow pain. You hassle me again? I'm not going to plead. Let us move to the deer. The deer were a nuisance. So They created a holding pen of blue glass. I mean They gathered porridge into piles of books and spatulas and paradises. The deer came to eat the porridge, and the deer packed up, tied cross-legged to face one another. Someone labeled the entire thing, titled it *Crunchy*, placed the transparent cube of deer inside the Panic City square and charged to pass the velvet ropes, to press the hot glass (you tap, you die). The deer had this look about them: *One day you fall asleep and next wake up in a labyrinth.* The girl took me deep. She needed someone to rub her eyes, and so yes, I rubbed her eyes. Now we sleep in moving water. We lie in any stream and feel the gurgling, below us, with our blood; the press of tiny, rounded stones along our vertebrae. They took her leg. My vocal cords. We look hard into the night sky. We strain to claim something. I rub her eyes. She says for both of us: "None of this is constellation. Saying doesn't make it so."

[an entire life

peeling by]

A Celebrity Pens a Letter Concerning Collage

a puzzle all mixed up the day my ma and pa left they rode off motorcycle it was blowing a blue sky like fore a storm my grandpa drank then and he don't drink since the big war never talks listen he has a folden shovel in the shop their a little log knife with an eagle on the handel we not even pop bubbles from gum cause mee maw says he can speak japaneese i never don't know he want tell no one grandpa drank wiskey and yelled out the yard he clumb the magnolia tree he hugged me tight the rain was big white blanket he said no blood would be tossed out a newspaper rolled up like that i was his son now was going to cry one time he told a story his lamint day he had to shoot two dogs chasing deer were eating fawns them hole had to shoot them and called them and sat with tongues out smiling and he shot them both he said was a mistake there and he was bible sad i said didn't you have to and he said no a person doesn't have to my parents lower than them dead dogs i did not see remember all the crows doing crazy circls they sounded like tin cans my uncle is my best friend now my uncle is my brother

[liberty bell is liberty bell
way cracked

honk! honk!—excuse me, your kneecap fell off
back there
cocksucker!]

goose

Vacate

And they feel exactly what at this debarking moment? I do not mean debarking. I mean they sit at a table and stare silent for hours. Moist and blue, the eyes. The bay window, the yawning beach, its rustling copper breeze.

"All we talk about is Elvis."

"No, no that's not gospel."

"It is gospel. We've become one of those people."

"No. We shook all last night."

(Between them tilts a stack of Popped Tarts)

"That isn't talking."

"We discussed our vacation. We were going to head down south…"

With a screech, the sun unhinges and falls into the ocean. It is the hiss of a thousand curtains, of loose-limbed yesterdays. Toadstools of steam. The moon is now the sun, and in the night sky a glittering, gold record. Oh, how the world dances, but then faints and folds up gasping into sleep. Oh how the tides go frenzy, but then slack-out, collapse, a final wavelet, then porcelain, glaring sigh. A saucer of perfectly spilt milk. The people drifting to the beaches with their crazy straws. To lie down together. To suck.

Along this Road

[switches shriek. flash pop to pop pop
picking pixels from the pixie inside
the hum—like love—of you
lost. duck down. dropped key locked
so pay attention. scamper now]

FEEL US WHEN ALONE
BROOD TO THE LAST CHOP!
FREE RED CARPET
BASTE FATE, GUESS WILLING
FUCK THROUGH THE WALLS!
DO NOT BRING YOUR HAWK

*a celebrity pens a letter concerning
the last photo of the girl:*

[i lamint now OK. that day is not good
on me. that's all i know on that photo i
mean my perspctive. i am done]

A deer will walk the path of least resistance. A human is the same. Every crackle of intellect avoids the roadways. The country-side disrobes thinking. And they did format the deer at this time. My point in this line of pondering? You will find yourself on the road, the way lightning finds _____.

ACE-TASTIN MOTIVATIN!

Well, I say
to nobody

                                        [some new kid shows up on crutches
                                        and they take the crutches and fix them
                                        somehow to the flagpole rope and now
                                        the flag up there all tangling and bangling
                                        in crutches]

Code (Interrupted in Transit) [2]

Mary 9

Wish through the stepwise. Silk hatch. Sail the sail. You boat sink shortly. Chock. Romanticize. All of this a baby shark. Shape the. Charge. Knobby arm the cute. WRAT URPH. Dyed belief, dyed little. Far one-way hush. Feeling in left leg. Lost. Knobby arm. To do with oral habits. It, or why even? CATW AL K CATW AL KCATWAL. Fee Air is the slice one lays for bleeding oneself a limb opossum game. Chock aerate. The gills. Not the first time. Above stall, Fee musk rubble lope in the start of Them. Above stall, a calm Air, give shout. Lanky run vole shun, give shout roaches to Heaven, is the lesson/lemon cake. Impossible and without notice. Like dirt. Like stars. Like rock walls like. Webs. Like sharks. John and his mustache. Per unit. Like the needle of shells. Delivered by knives. Like lifting fog. TIE NOSSE HAVIAT. No human ever synthesized silk. Grow. Shark. Chock.

[like to kidney
throat slit open to allow. laughter 141423---]

Applaud

Like moths to chrome. What she always said, the first Hitting Coach. *You keep emphasizing the knees, but how do I look someone in the eye and…* "Like moths to chrome, and I never told knees. Or eyes. I told kneecaps." Oh, the first Hitting Coach would go sullen, would climb a tree and perch in the windowsill and maybe smoke a mixture of crushed fingernails and popcorn in a copper bowl. (Once, a blue moth flew into her mouth.) The second Hitting Coach was 14 years old and too honest. The third Hitting Coach obsessed over electricity. At this point, the entire Program tottering. Would there even be a fourth Hitting Coach? Most days we stand in light rain like lost cattle, masting, with the huddled. Masting is when we search for nuts: hickory, pecan, black walnuts. From forest floor to grind their bones to knead a type of flapjack. Walnuts are a tough nut, and Lucille Ball brings a ball peen hammer, a claw hammer, a sledge hammer hitched to two ponies with wide white eyes like peonies, I mean to say blooming. "Every single thing is posture. All of you balance a walnut atop your head." Lucille unbuckles the sledge from the harness and hands me the hammer, my gods its weight, my gods the surprising Laws of earth. Lucille clutches my shoulder, digs in, laps loopy eyelashes; says, "You are going to be funny and loved now, kid. Just watch."

Race Road

The flyover was incorrect. I clearly remember peaches (or spiders?) dropping from the sky the sickening splat
the runners slipping in their crying juices.

I admired the somersault of a child.

OK, trampled. Crushed like a little water cup. (We are allowed to litter during the event.)

Someone do something!

Yes, I:

1. checked my big watch.
2. sucked a shard of hard candy.
3. imagined a little man in my forehead who sat on a tall chair and controlled my lungs and legs with a series of gyroscopes, levers, and gears.

Oh, observe her big, brass, glittering medal
(its ribbon made of baby eels).

[soon dried up
expired/born into
bookmarks]

The First War

She was kneeling on the bunker roof and copying what she knew about love into a folder: A PUMPKIN SO SIMPLE FIRST THEN SOMEONE JACK-O-LANTERNS CARVES A MADE FACE SPIKE OF FIRE THE BRAIN MONTHS LATER ELBOW SWEAT OF FOREST FACE SAGGING TENDERNESS GRAY-GREEN COLLAPSE. People learn to sleep while walking, while framing memories of horse races. She wants to make a serious wager. She wants to feel good while losing. Look, a photo of an empty suit of armor, painfully bent over, (trying to read a bronze palm?), the tears of Body left behind, the rust preparing double screwdrivers, drunk through a straw. You guessed it—she and Franz Ferdinand rode mules across precipices of poppy flowers. The air told them nothing matters. Yes, they fell in love. It happens every day. (I can't really observe anything about the wind, unless I see something fluttering, bent, something moving that is not the wind.) What happened? They started censoring hips. Bent minds to tin and squeamish bedtimes. Sought out vex. They gnawed those silent dinners that will overfish an hour and Time falls into chalky fingers of stone, brown mosslings like deflated… They started a world war, didn't they? You love long enough and both become the other—face, habits, taunts, thoughts—a cliché drip, drip and dry. Franz Ferdinand, the instant before the gun-crack: he looked alone.

Hell

As you tri-articulate the cinder tunnels toss your gray, knit cap into the air. Catch the cap in scorched hand. Often the cap spins on axis of an outstretched finger. Like a red monsoon. Like a melting, silent film. Reel to reel. Like you are pain dancing.

[the veterans

cough]

Firing Squad

—Do you have any last wishes?

—Yes, I do. I would like a ceiling fan. I enjoy the white noise of a ceiling fan.

[they sold out
of thick shawls
chewing gum
frisbees
and a rumple-box of
floating bones]

Momentum

We almost ate a fashionable hat! It was glossy and bruised. We thought grape jelly. Grape jelly on the abdomen of a rotted log. The log lay across the creek at the oddest angle—imagine a bloody jawbone clutching the elbow of a pillow. A certain type of hunger and everything resembles food. There was great debate and head-purging. Hurtful verbs were shouldered and flung. Comments on noses and internal inertia. One of us said, "Touch it with the Stimulator." Another said, "The problem is we have no blind seeker. If we had a blind seeker like a respectable…" It was crazy talk, sure, but have you struck hunger? Forest stones with faces, veins, blood. A shriveled apple with penetrating eye-sockets, pupils to pluck. Or maybe suck the heavy marrow from Styrofoam worms (and this just a summary, a metonym of our days). Ended up, it was fungi. Great globs of shimmering purple fungi. Later that season Yves St. Laurent would smoke 150 cigarettes per day and collect all the fungi and place them lopsided atop the wealthy ladies' heads. The look was perfect, it was noted, as if grown there.

Chilly and Feeling Weak

A glass bowl of disposable lighters. A bowl of fireworks. A little wind-up dog. An altar made of still-warm meat yet hung. Glass stains. Bears with crosses. Curtains ironing the waxes out of candles. In the words of all: "The prayer of continuing any act simply because we started the act, Amen." A gilded sling shot. Fact: Not one person saved. Fact: I enjoy the swish of rain sweeping a roof, most any roof, and so attended gloomy days. Fact: Velvet is a tangled clod. Fact: All over the world. Fact: Relentless and horrible rain. Fact: A philosophy of quietism. Fact: Ugly contrasts. Fact: Urns and earns, a form of learning. Fact: Instability. Fact: An old-fashioned coward. Fact: A walk now and then, a falling forward. Fact: An underwater house. Fact: A neon sign above the two bowls. Fact: It read SHARE.

[technology is lonely

a properly folded flag impossible to unfold

without major damage]

A Multidisciplinary Approach to Obesity

The deer are pulling. *Tethers*. The trains are slow, hunched men of hot gold. I mean to say we faint at our own reflections as the trains go hobbling by, big woods, bigger and older than the World, over there, gone, splayed out like a starlit/split *carcassi*. Hillside of bones/discarded philosophies/funky smudges/durations/nightmares/mind openers of Flee Wheel. Smoke like music on the air. I'll tell you the truth: *derailment, fluvial, quondam, tepefy*. Or I am tired of my religion. Also fishy handshakes. Limp verbs. Things do fall apart. It is radical now to actually talk. The word *polite* has killed more human beings than any _____. By and by…Brain as ellipsis. Semen the same. Eggs. Silent dinners. Most everything dry. The fish have been stilled. The flowers melted into revolvers. They did what? Took all the _____ and jellied them and rolled them into flapjacks. DIE THE ENDLY FLY. It just {lie} dawned on me: all of us are digging. At our particular miles per hour. 14, 23, 5, 9—for my friends. What friends? Identify strategies to kiss the ground/genuflect/sweep the tile veranda/promote illness. I forgot about the odor of rotting storytellers. Fallen words. Cockroaches fly very well. Darwin's bathtub, for example. You should go home. You should witness unbelievable airborne activity. This is serious. But you'll never {?} say so. What? I forgot to tell you that God has left us; She now huddles curled inside every poor play of chess {all}. Fallen leaflets. Look around. Shut up. We have people in the North. We sing fondly of hell. So. I said *drink*. Take a slow breath. Listen. To this God: *I see*, She whispered, and saw nothing.

[here i mean

you

me

fact: rosy tornado of shit

like we was placed wrong
ain't no reply
grandpa says
a man can't punch a big system]

cell phone = walkie-talkie

suv = tonka truck

latte = milkshake

Over 2500 left handed people a year killed
from using products made
4 right handed people

yawn

[to halt Death
tell a cow to halt
standing dumbly in the
rain]

coffee?

Free: Blue Hanging Folders

—I dropped off to sleep or off the earth.

—I know I saw Agatha Christie.

—I know I lost my sole and thought: I hope no one notices I lost my sole. I limped on, I shuffled. A young lady approached and said, "You lost your sole."

—My labor was prolonged, then nearly skilled, as is my way.

—What I must do is a mystery.

—I give your commitment one year, she said.

—Why did you…they say?

—Disappear.

—To run the road of reflection is my undoing. I'll admit that. You are my "friend" the way a smiling predator is happiness.

—I fish myself.

—Example: Would you hark to move a picture/thin mints/drag a shallow lake? Well, hire me. (This was during Septembers of employment. They now call us mollycoddled.)

—I might have started a boyish fashion but I was a boy.

—Oh, I came of age.

　　　　　　　　　　　　　　[…blocking out the affixed subjects with his thumb, still tentative, despite the cultivated naturalism of this wonderful scene…]

—A box of my own devising and I tried to fill the box with things.

—I spun thin carpet so I could murmur thick carpet.

—This bed that clicked and groaned.

—I moved for you. Etc.

—Oh, the days I longed for quiet beds.

—The moving pictures were the handy thing, as I earlier…

within the box of my own devising:

[a bluebird flew into the window and S drank a
beer. There is a giant on the roof! "there's a giant
amount of snow you mean," said H. H drank
a beer and S drank a beer. H drank a beer. H
lives across the tracks/down the street from S
and retired from a lifetime of Y and a lifetime of
Y stock and then Y went under like a fly to the
hammering shoe and now H comes to S's kitchen
table and they sit and listen to all the objects
picked, dropped, fancied by the wind. S drank a
beer. H drank a beer. H said, "James Brown had
150 kids and he left them nothing." H drank a
beer. S drank a beer. S heard a lobster crawling
across the window, these little etchings of feet.
S drank a beer. H said the rug was incredibly
orange. "whoever dyed that rug did a fine job and

respected his hands and knees and the energy of his life he gifted. a rug is useful thing." S drank a beer. a fox with three legs passed the window. H drank a beer. H said, "James Brown would only fuck in the missionary position. Didn't know there was another way." the snow was pale blue in the moonlight. S drank a beer. H drank a beer. a sound like un-popped corn kernels and H stood and toppled over, down the railroad, into the blur of snow curling high into shadowy mounds—i mean into his home]

—*How did it happen?*

—Fugitive dust.

—Every problem can be traced to this: someone thinks.

—One day scales were faced, another madness banished and islands felled, mostly landing in the streets and tumbling, the palm trunks splintering into chicken bones, the sand castles shaking clear of sand.

—After every holiday a natural disaster.

—I do regret the consumers.

—The day is drawing apart at the corners.

—And the peat bog. That was prohibitive.

—I listen without trembling.

—Hot pants and long legs, trends I did not comprehend.

—I woke to coughing down the hallway. I crept through the bog, into the Living Room. There tottered an old man atop my television set—he had long legs and hot pants. He said, "My name is Robert Frost and I am wise in a simple way and depressed in a happy way and I am the first poet to be on your TV."

—I remember…

[bluebirds hanging by their own tongues]

—I remember little, due to closed head injury, bluebirds, and broken frames—my youth escaped again, the car parked on the cliff's edge

the body gone.

Having Fun in Spring

By Jenna Lee Gleisner

Picture Glossary

3

It is spring.

I see rain.

rain

It is spring.

I see a puddle.

umbrella

It is spring.

I see leaves.

leaves

It is spring.

I see flowers.

flowers

It is spring.

I see baby birds.

birds

Do You Know?

What is he holding?

rain

puddle

umbrella

leaves

flowers

birds